SO-BDH-219

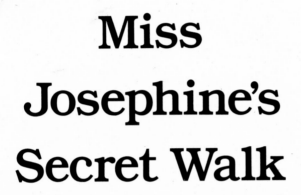

Miss
Josephine's
Secret Walk

by Yuji Kobayashi

THE GREEN TIGER PRESS
San Diego
1987

"Oh what a beautiful morning!", says Miss Josephine as she slips out of bed.

She splashes her face with water, does her morning business, and trims her whiskers to make a pretty face.

Puff, puff. She puts on powder.

A touch of lipstick.
A red necklace.
Mother's skirt and hat.

"I feel so elegant.
I must go out."

Agnes sees her, grabs her skirt, and
Miss Josephine tumbles head over
heels.

"Oh Josephine, I'm so sorry," says Agnes.
Little Katy says, "Let's all play together."

They start walking, and as they cross
a bridge they sing,

"Log bridge, log bridge—well, well, well.
Log bridge, log bridge—well, well, well."

WHOOSH!

The water is cold, but it's fun. The three friends float down the river together.

They ride over the waterfall.
Miss Josephine's necklace
breaks and the beads fly all
around.

They shine like drops of dew.

The red beads are now wild berries.
They smell good and taste good:
a little sweet and a little sour.

"It's getting dark!
Let's hurry home!"

Their mothers and fathers are all
waiting together, and are very worried!
"Where have you been?"
The three friends answer:
"We can't tell! It's our secret!"

The text is set in Bookman by Professional Typography of San Diego, California
Printed and bound in Hong Kong

Original Japanese edition published by
Fukutake Publishing Co., Ltd., Tokyo, Japan 1986
USAGI NO ELNA-CHAN HIMITSU NO SAMPO by Yuji Kobayashi
Copyright © Yuji Kobayashi 1986
English Translation Arranged with Fukutake Publishing Co., Ltd.,
2-3-28 Kudanminami, Chiyoda-ku, Tokyo, Japan